Into the Unknown

Anastacia Dikih

Paperback: 978-1-967820-66-5
Hardcover: 978-1-967820-68-9
eBook: 978-1-967820-67-2
Library of Congress Control Number: 2025910321

This is a work of fiction.

Ordering Information:

Prime Seven Media
518 Landmann St.
Tomah City, WI 54660

Printed in the United States of America

For my children and their children

Author Anastacia Dikih 2023

Illustrator Anastacia Dikih 2023
Copyrighted

"Don't turn us in!!"
shouted Boris running after
the third mate.

"Now we're doomed!"
exclaimed Nikita.

"What shall we do now?"
said Arkadi as they watched
in disbelief.

The boys had made plans
before the trip began but
now, they were discovered.
What went wrong?

Boris, Nikita and Arkadi were friends.
They finished their training as sailors at
a Navy University on an island north of
Japan. Boris was a tall lad with wavy brown
hair, as he was working on the ship, he wore a
stripped blue shirt.

Nikita also had brown hair, but he wore a
purple shirt and Arkadi wore a green shirt.

Boris came from a city by the Ural
mountains. Where Nikita and Arkadi were
from central part of Russia.

"Hello! Can I speak with Arkadi?" asked Boris.

"He's not on the bridge right now,
can I take a message for him?" answered Nikita.

"Sure," replied Boris.

"I would like to meet up with Arkadi at a cafe on shore as my ship is heading out to Canada to get some grain.

Could you please pass on this message?" Boris asked.

"Sure," answered Nikita.

Nikita was excited after the phone call he received
from Boris. He had an idea that he wanted to share
with Boris and Arkadi. Over dinner he laid out his
plan of leaving the country by hiding in the ship
that Boris was working on.

Bursting with excitement Nikita blurted out over dinner.

"I want to move to another country and try someplace new." "You got to be crazy!" exclaimed Arkadi.

"How do you plan on doing this?" asked Boris.

"Easy," said Nikita. "Hide in your ship and jump ship when we get to Canada," "Are you serious, Nikita!" exclaimed the other boys.

"Why not, what have we to lose?" answered Nikita.

Coffee

Late into the night the boys discussed this idea and looked at it from different angles. Going over each point so that they would not make the wrong decision. They also considered the chance of getting caught and the consequences of their actions.

Next morning Nikita woke up
with a start. He made a serious
decision last night that he didn't
take lightly. He packed his stuff
everything that he needed for his
trip to Canada.

He went and found Arkadi. He was
still in bed and didn't want to go
but Nikita convinced him that it
was a good idea to go. Together
they got ready their stuff and
joined Boris in his cabin after
they gave their passport at the
entrance.

17

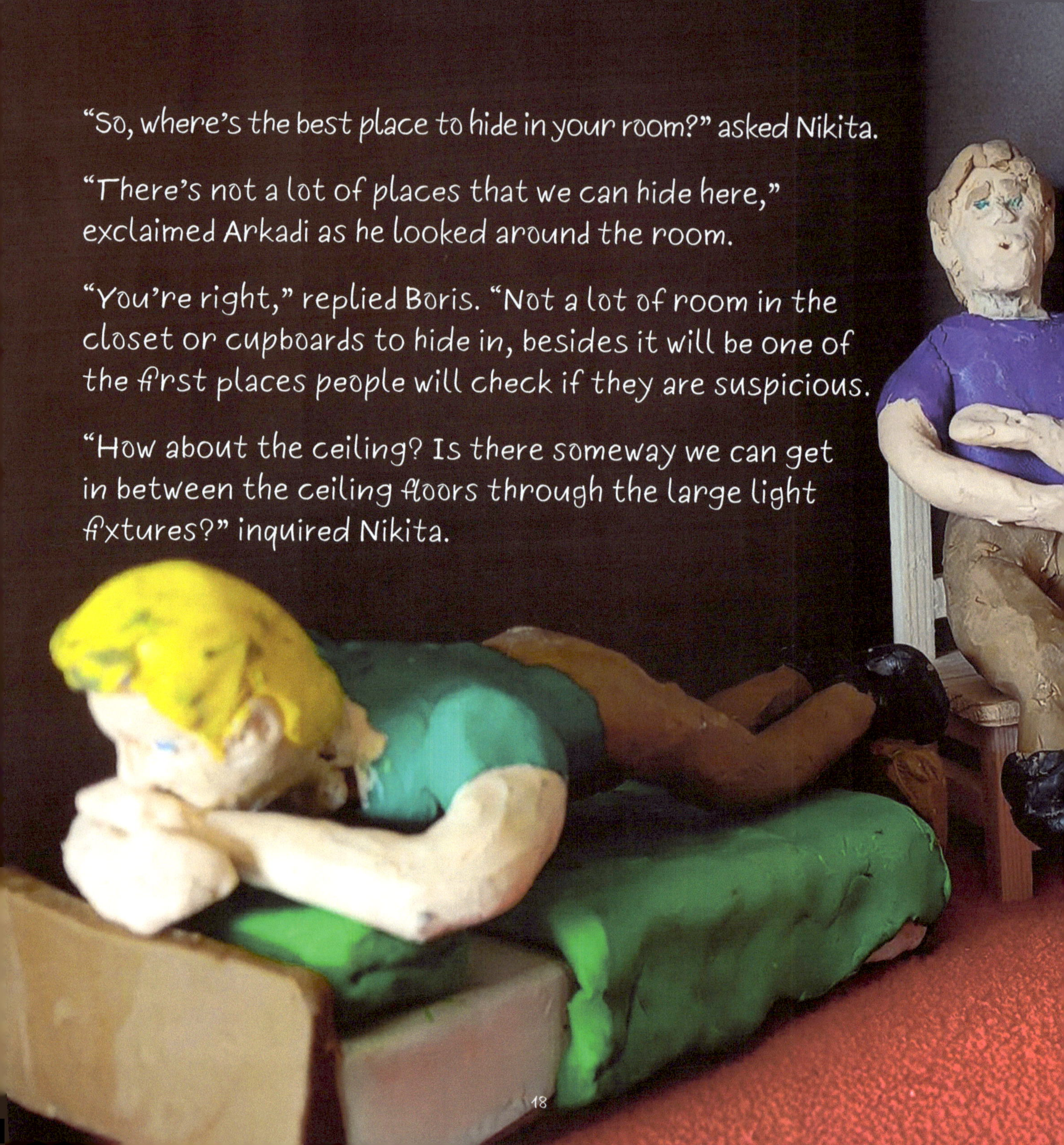

"So, where's the best place to hide in your room?" asked Nikita.

"There's not a lot of places that we can hide here," exclaimed Arkadi as he looked around the room.

"You're right," replied Boris. "Not a lot of room in the closet or cupboards to hide in, besides it will be one of the first places people will check if they are suspicious.

"How about the ceiling? Is there someway we can get in between the ceiling floors through the large light fixtures?" inquired Nikita.

"Let's give it a try," replied Boris as he
unscrewed the light fixture and the boys
climbed in.

"This will work for us here," said Nikita from
within the opening.

The boys were excited and nervous at the same time. Sasha came to visit Boris on his ship. He was surprised at their plan and told them that they were insane. He pointed out the consequences of their choice and tried to persuade them to change their minds. Boris, Nikita and Arkadi never waivered in their decision and laughed at the fears of their visiting friend. Sasha was the last person to see them as they left for Canada, and he was the first person among their friends to see Nikita ten years later.

An announcement was
heard over the loudspeaker.
It was informing all friends
and family to disembark, as
the crew were getting ready
to set sail on their journey
to Canada.

Sasha tried once more to
change his friend's mind
about leaving their country.
Boris, Nikita and Arkadi
refused to listen and with
a heavy heart Sasha said his
goodbyes. Wishing them
success and smooth sailing,
he left the cabin. Sasha
picked up his passport on
his way off the ship, he never
told anyone what his friends
were doing.

"How are we going to get our passports?" inquired Arkadi.

"I've decided to give the sailor on duty a five-minute break to fetch some lunch. This way I can grab your passports without any suspicion. When your passports are gone everyone will think that all visitors have left the ship." Informed Boris.

"Sounds like a good plan," said Nikita.

With that Boris left the cabin to retrieve the passports. On his return he was holding their passport and giving it to them he said,

"Here are your documents, put them in a safe place."

The first part of their plan worked out for now there were a few more hurdles to overcome.

"Let's get you into your hiding places as officials will be coming around asking questions.

I've taken a shift on the bridge right now to avoid being nervous when they ask questions,"

Boris informed them while he unscrewed the light fixture and waited for the boys to climb in.

As soon as he secured the light fixture Boris left the cabin and the boys were left with their minds racing.

In his hiding place Nikita had to calm his nerves. He said the Lord's prayer a few times then added a personal petition to the God above.

"Please protect us and help us arrive to Canada safely, thanks in advance. Amen," prayed Nikita.

Nikita was full of anxiety, worried of getting caught and ending up in jail. There was no turning back now, what was going to happen will happen anyway thought Nikita as he waited in anticipation. From exhaustion he soon fell asleep. After a few hours of sleep Nikita woke up and listened to his surroundings. He heard the ship's engines working and he realized they were on there way to Canada. Nobody found them, they were safe for now. It was quiet in the cabin below as Boris was still working his shift.

For the next little bit, the
boys took all precautions
and came down only during
the night when most people
were sleeping. They ate,
stretched their legs and
took care of their personal
needs. Most of the time
they spent their days up in
the ceiling and came down
only during the night.

As time went by the boys
became braver, they
started having louder
conversation and came
down out of their hiding
place earlier in the evening.
Soon their bravery would be
tested.

One evening when Nikita and Arkadi were
out from their hiding place to have some
food and discussing Boris's activities
during the day. They heard a knock on the
door and in a panic the boys climbed into
the nearest cabinets under the counters.

Boris went and answered the door, in
piled a group of guys each excited to have
some fun during the evening hours. Boris
was anxious but didn't show it. He would
rather they left him alone but if he asked
them to leave, the guys might become
suspicious. He wanted none of that, so he
pretended to have fun and interacted with
his guests.

Meanwhile Nikita and Arkadi were cramped
in the cabinet trying not to reveal
themselves to the guests in the room.

As the boys' fingertips grew numb from the pressure of holding the door closed and their legs were about to give up from their cramped position. They waited impatiently for the guests to leave.

After a few hours of conversation, the guests left for the night, and it wasn't a moment too soon. "That was longer than I thought it would be," exclaimed Nikita as he straightens out his cramped legs. "Well, that serves us right for not being careful," noted Arkadi as he climbed out of the cabinet.

"I definitely will not be inviting those guys again," sighed Boris in relief as they prepared themselves for the night each going to their own place.

That was a close call.

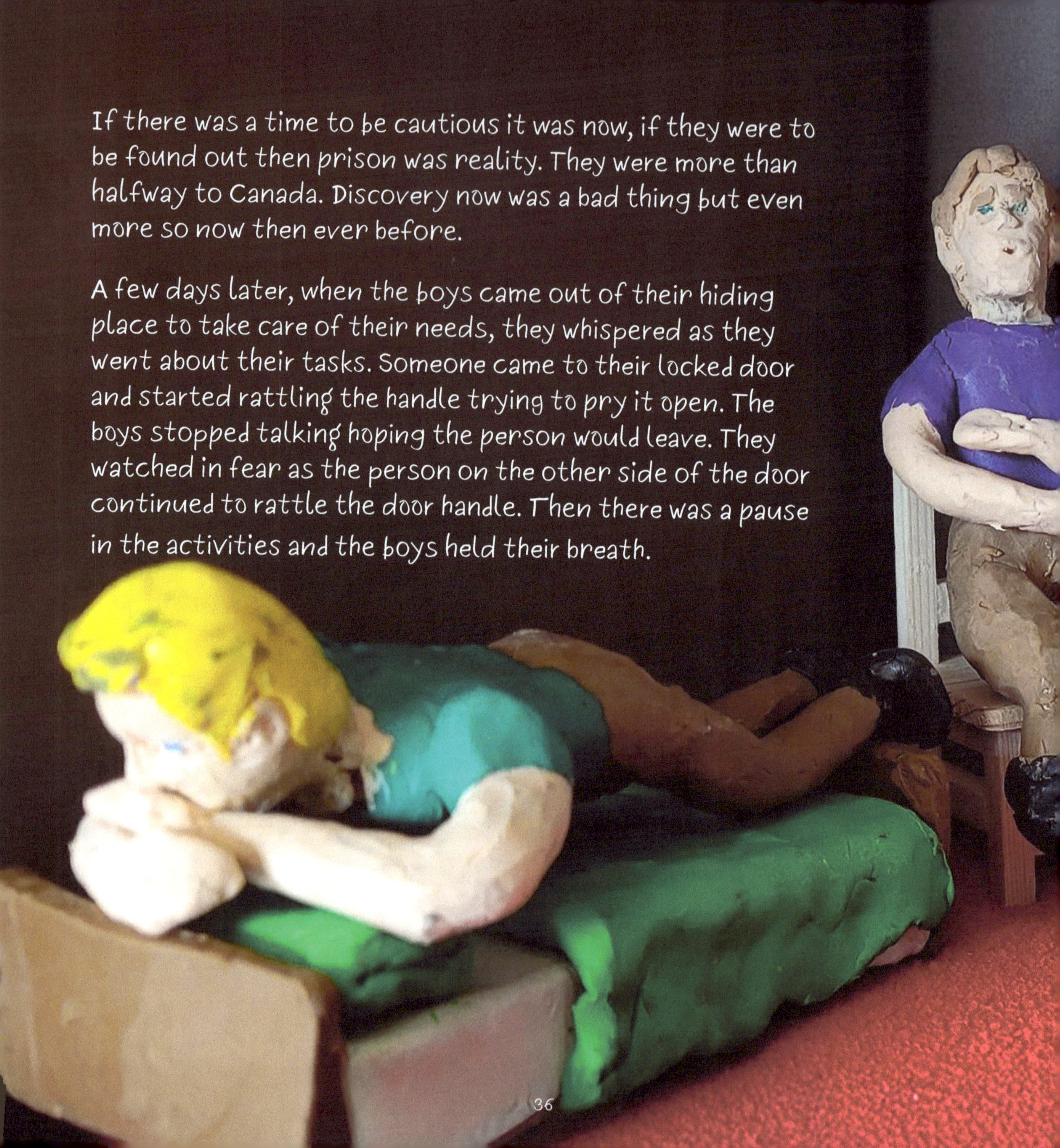

If there was a time to be cautious it was now, if they were to be found out then prison was reality. They were more than halfway to Canada. Discovery now was a bad thing but even more so now then ever before.

A few days later, when the boys came out of their hiding place to take care of their needs, they whispered as they went about their tasks. Someone came to their locked door and started rattling the handle trying to pry it open. The boys stopped talking hoping the person would leave. They watched in fear as the person on the other side of the door continued to rattle the door handle. Then there was a pause in the activities and the boys held their breath.

What was going to happen? Will they be discovered? What will they do if they are found? These thoughts raced through the boys' minds.

A few seconds went by as they
waited. Then with a turn of the door
handle the door stood wide open.
They were exposed as the third
mate was standing in the doorway.
Everyone stood still taking in
what just happened. Then the third
mate turned on his heels and fled
down the hallway. Boris jumped into
action running after the guy.

He shouted, "Don't turn us in!!"
The other boys in the cabin were
speechless, they had no strength
to move their limbs in shock. Their
worst fear became reality, what
now? What should they do?

"Grab your stuff and be ready to run at moment notice," Boris informed the boys. "Where shall we run?" inquired Arkadi.

"We can put up a fight if they come after us," said Nikita as he moved to grab his things. "We're not going to giving up this easy!" continued Nikita.

"Let's not panic for now, in the meantime lets get you into your hiding spots," informed Boris as he moved to unscrew the light fixture.

With these instructions the boys climbed into the ceiling expecting the captain to arrive at any moment to arrest them. As the evening wore on, each person wrestled with his thoughts. They all had a hard time falling asleep. A few prayers were heard during the night as each person fell asleep in exhaustion and turmoil. It was a restless night for them all.

The next morning Boris had a shift and with deep rooted fear he went to his position on the bridge. The third mate avoided eye contact making Boris even more nervous than he already was. The morning wore on and the tension was tense with each second. Some time went by, and the captain called Boris to his desk. He slowly approached the desk expecting the worst.

The captain asked Boris, "What's the English word for this instrument?" he inquired pointing to a compass on the desk. Boris was lost for words and stood still in disbelief. The captain repeated the question again then laughed. "Student! Don't they teach you anything in school? Boris, you need to know these things in English if you want to get ahead," informed the captain as he sent Boris back to his station shaking his head in disbelief at the lack of knowledge of the recruit.

Boris sighed a breath of relief; he realized that the third mate had not said anything to the captain and wondered why.

The next few days there was a mood of excitement on board. The crew were informed that they were drawing near to land. For the crew on board, it was a time of intense activities in preparation to receive grain to take back to their country.

For the stowaway boys it was a time of intense anticipation of the final steps on leaving the ship to start new life.

The next day, an Island came into view, they passed it
and headed straight to port as they were empty. They
came to the grain station and docked for the night.
Tomorrow morning the ship will be loaded up with grain.

The boys in the cabin waited until the next day to make
their move, as they were still in danger of getting
arrested.

The next day the boys got their stuff together and prepare to leave the ship. They waited until it was lunchtime before going out into the open, they would be exposing themselves to those on board the ship.

"Let's go through the tunnel to the edge of the ship," Boris informed Nikita and Arkadi. "This way we can meet less people along the way," continued Boris.

"I'm ready to go," piped Arkadi nervously.

"It's now or never," responded Nikita as he moved in behind Arkadi as they followed Boris who was leading them out of the cabin.

They surfaced on deck and ran to the edge of the ship and jumped overboard onto the dock. The ship was over two stories high, two of the boys badly bruised their legs. Nikita landed on his duffle bag, and he didn't get bruised. They couldn't stop now as they thought someone would come after them, but no one did.

"We made it!" exclaimed Nikita as they passed a vending machine. To him it indicated that they have arrived in the city without going through customs.

They spent their first night in a park downtown expecting to be arrested at any moment, but this didn't happen.

The next morning, they discussed what they should do.

"What should we get for breakfast?" asked Boris.

"Let's first find out how much it costs to rent a room for the night," said Nikita.

"First let's assess how much money we have. If we have only $200 amongst us, we'll need to be careful how we spend it," said Arkadi.

"Let's ask around and find out what we can. How good is your English boys?" inquired Boris.

The boys walked about town asking questions in their limited and broken English those questions they discussed earlier.

"It will cost us $80 to rent out a room for one night at the hotel!" exploded Nikita in disbelief.

"Even breakfast at McDonalds costs $3.99 not to mention anything about how much it costs for lunch and dinner!" exclaimed Boris.

"We need to watch how we spend our money here; it's not going to be easy," informed Arkadi.

They sat down on a bench to think things through. This is one step the boys didn't thinks about when they headed out more than two weeks ago. There had to be a way out for them as they got up to continued walking around town.

That evening they found an all-night café and sat down at a table ordering just coffee the whole night through.

"I guess we can only order coffee for now," said Arkadi as he sat down at a table.

"I hope no one makes a big deal about it," answered Boris as he is joining them at the table. "No need to draw attention to ourselves," piped in Nikita as he grabbed the menu.

The waiter was a new immigrant from Mexico. He worked night shifts on the weekends because he was going to school to get his degree in hospitality.

He took pity on the boys and approached them with a piece of paper understanding what must be going on their minds right now.

"Hi fellas, how are you?" asked Pedro the waiter. "I noticed that you've been ordering only coffee tonight. Are you new to Canada? Is there some way I could help you out," continued Pedro.

In broken English the boys were afraid to share too much information, but they needed help. Finally, they understood what Pedro was offering. Pedro gave them an address to Mosaic community that helped immigrants get settled in Canada.

The next day the boys found their way to Mosaic based on the directions given by Pedro. It was a different part of the town, and not downtown. The boys had to take the Skytrain to the location as it was too far to walk on foot. Entering the building they asked at the front desk if someone was available to help them. They were lead down the hallway to a room on the right, where they were introduced to Polina.

"Good day boys, have a sit, how can I help you," spoke Polina in their language.

"At last! we don't have to rack our brain with our limited English to express ourselves," exclaimed Nikita.

"We jumped ship a few days ago and want to start life anew in this country," informed Boris as he sat down into the nearest chair and the others followed.

"Our English is poor, and financially we're limited. What are our options to get settled?" asked Arkadi.

"Well, I can help you here. Mosaic helps by providing newcomers with opportunity for employment, English classes, legal info and more," informed them Polina.

"Cool!" exclaimed the boys as they sighed in relief.

Polina helped them to fill out the forms for welfare, arranged English classes they can attend and gave them the address to a hostel where they can spend the night.

www.translink.ca
074
Please Stand Back Until Passengers Exit

That week was a busy one for the boys. They attended English classes, went to the immigration office for work permits and checked out a few rentals with Polina. Based on their combined welfare income they had enough money to pay for their rent and were able to use the rest of the money on personal things. The day came when they were able to move into their new place.

"This is so cool!" exclaimed Nikita looking around their newly furnished suite. They each had their own room with everything they needed to be comfortable.

"Who knew if it was possible!" voiced Boris.

"Yeah, I can buy myself some cool cloths!" added Arkadi, putting on his new sports jacket that he bought earlier in the day.

Life for our heroes started off on a positive note, now it was up to them to make it work.

THE END